Also in the *Meet* . . . series

And look out for more *Meet* . . . books coming soon

Meet...

BANJO PATERSON

WRITTEN BY KRISTIN WEIDENBACH

ILLUSTRATED BY JAMES GULLIVER HANCOCK

RANDOM HOUSE AUSTRALIA

For my mum, Jennifer, who loves 'Clancy of the Overflow'. KW

For all my Australian family and friends. JGH

A Random House book
Published by Random House Australia Pty Ltd
Level 3, 100 Pacific Highway, North Sydney NSW 2060
www.randomhouse.com.au

First published by Random House Australia in 2015

National Library of Australia
Cataloguing-in-Publication Entry

Author: Weidenbach, Kristin
Title: Meet Banjo Paterson/Kristin Weidenbach; James Gulliver Hancock, illustrator
ISBN: 978 0 85798 008 3 (hbk)
Series: Meet; 7.
Target Audience: For children.
Subjects: Paterson, Andrew Barton, 1864–1941 – Juvenile literature.
Poets, Australian – 20th century – Juvenile literature.
Pioneers – Australia – Juvenile literature.
Other Authors/Contributors: Hancock, James Gulliver, illustrator
Dewey Number: A821.2

Cover and internal design by Kirby Armstrong
Printed and bound in China by 1010 Printing International Limited

BANJO PATERSON is one of Australia's most loved poets. This is the story of how he came to write his legendary ballads 'The Man from Snowy River' and 'Waltzing Matilda'.

Banjo Paterson loved horses.

He learned to ride when he was six years old. Every morning he would catch his pony in the paddock and bring him into the yard. After breakfast he would ride six kilometres to school. At the end of the day he rode six kilometres home again.

Everyone rode horses back then. The mail came in a coach pulled by horses. Families travelled from Sydney or Melbourne in horse-drawn wagons.

Banjo would stand by the roadside and study the teams of bullocks and horses that passed by. He loved the jangle of the spurs and the crack of the stockwhips.

At the annual town races near Yass, Banjo watched the horses prance in their stalls. He tasted the dust as they dashed past in a cloud of thundering hooves.

Banjo loved life in the outback. He loved the shearers and stockmen, who wore hats and braces and swapped yarns around the campfire. He loved the leathery smell of the saddles and stirrups and saddlebags. He loved the velvety tickle of a foal's nose.

When Banjo grew up, he worked as a lawyer in Sydney. But his heart belonged to the bush.

As he sat in his dingy office, Banjo dreamed of the drovers bringing big mobs of cattle down from Queensland. He stared out the window and longed to swap places with those in the back of beyond.

For the drover's life has pleasures that the
townsfolk never know . . .

And in place of lowing cattle, I can hear the
fiendish rattle

Of the tramways and the buses making
hurry down the street . . .

Little by little, Banjo began to write about the outback life he yearned for. He wrote a poem about a drover called Clancy. When his poem was published, people said it was one of the best bush ballads they had ever heard.

Banjo wrote more poems about horses and horsemen and horse races. He wrote about polo matches and bushrangers and jockeys.

He wrote about a man called Mulga Bill, who boasted that riding a bicycle was just like riding a horse.

’Twas Mulga Bill, from Eaglehawk, that caught
the cycling craze;
He turned away the good old horse that
served him many days…

But a bike is not like a horse, as Mulga Bill found out. It bolted away down the hill, dodging trees and wallabies before it hit a rock and sprang into the air. Mulga Bill let out a piercing shriek as he flew over the handlebars and into Dead Man’s Creek.

Banjo’s poems were funny and exciting.

SALTBUSH BILL
CLANCY
THE MAN FROM SNOWY RIVER

Banjo wrote about Saltbush Bill and The Man from Ironbark. But it was the ballad about The Man from Snowy River that made him famous. The poem told of how a station pony ran away to join a mob of wild horses. All the stockmen and drovers in the district tried to catch it – even the drover named Clancy.

But only The Man from Snowy River, galloping his horse across steep gorges and gullies, was able to round up the mob.

He sent the flint stones flying, but the pony kept his feet,
He cleared the fallen timber in his stride,
And the man from Snowy River never shifted in his seat –
It was grand to see that mountain horseman ride.

Banjo's book of poems about The Man from Snowy River and other outback characters sold out within a week. It was an Australian record. People passed the poems around from city to bush.

Banjo's name was on everyone's lips.

Banjo stayed at a friend's sheep station in Queensland to escape all the fuss. There, he learned of a swagman who drowned in a waterhole while running from the police. Banjo saw a dead sheep nearby and wondered if it had been killed by the swagman.

As these images rolled around in Banjo's head, a new poem began to form. He called it 'Waltzing Matilda', which means 'to carry a swag'.

When music was added to Banjo's poem, the famous song was born.

Once a jolly swagman camped by a billabong,
Under the shade of a coolibah tree . . .
And his ghost may be heard as you pass by that billabong,
You'll come a-waltzing Matilda with me!

The song travelled by word of mouth around the country. Every Australian soon knew about the jolly swagman whose ghost haunted the billabong under a coolibah tree.

Banjo's writing conjured up the scent of gum trees and the crackling of a campfire. His poems were recited from the backs of horses as drovers followed their stock. They were passed around in shearing sheds from one bushie to another.

Banjo loved the Australian outback and, as long as he had a pen and paper, he would never stop writing about it.

TIMELINE

1864 (17 February): Andrew Barton Paterson is born in Narrambla, New South Wales. His family call him Barty.

1871: When Barty is seven years old, his family move to a station called Illalong, in the Snowy Mountains region near Yass. Barty rides his pony to the one-teacher school in Binalong.

1872: The rouseabout at Illalong takes eight-year-old Barty to the local horse races. One of the riders borrows Barty's saddle and wins the main race. Many years later, the incident inspires Paterson to write the poem 'Old Pardon, the Son of Reprieve'.

1875: Barty moves to Sydney to live with his grandmother and attend Sydney Grammar School. Instead of hobnailed boots and moleskins, he has to wear good clothes and behave like a young gentleman.

1881: When Barty finishes school, he starts work as a clerk and studies to become a lawyer.

1886 (June): Paterson's poem 'The Bush Fire' is published in *The Bulletin*. Instead of using his real name, he signs the poem as 'The Banjo', which is the name of a horse he used to ride.

1886 (August): Paterson begins work as a solicitor in Sydney.

1886 (October): *The Bulletin* publishes 'A Dream of the Melbourne Cup' by The Banjo. The editor of the magazine encourages Paterson to write about the bush.

1888: 'Old Pardon, the Son of Reprieve' is published in *The Bulletin*. It is the first of Paterson's characteristic bush ballads, or story poems. No one yet knows the real identity of The Banjo.

1889: 'Clancy of the Overflow' is published in the Christmas issue of *The Bulletin*. It is the first of Paterson's ballads to becoming widely popular.

1890: 'The Man from Snowy River' is published in *The Bulletin*.

1895: The Banjo's first book of poetry, *The Man from Snowy River and Other Verses*, is published in October. It sells out within a week and breaks an Australian publishing record. The Banjo becomes famous overnight, and Paterson's identity is revealed.

Paterson writes 'Waltzing Matilda' while visiting Dagworth Station, a sheep station near Winton, Queensland. It becomes Australia's unofficial national anthem.

1899: Paterson travels to South Africa for six months to cover the Boer War as a reporter.

1902: Paterson's second book of poetry, *Rio Grande's Last Race and Other Verses*, is published.

1903: Paterson is appointed editor of Sydney's *The Evening News*. He marries Alice Walker, and they go on to have two children, Grace and Hugh.

1903: Inglis & Co. adapt the music and lyrics of 'Waltzing Matilda' to promote the Billy Tea brand. This is the version sung today and reproduced in this book.

1906: *An Outback Marriage*, Paterson's first novel, is published.

1915: Paterson travels to Egypt as an Australian Army captain in World War I. He is a member of the Remount Unit, which trains and cares for the horses used by soldiers. He looks after 50,000 horses and 10,000 mules before returning to Australia in 1919, when the war is over. None of the horses come home.

1921: Paterson becomes editor of *The Sydney Sportsman*.

1930: Paterson retires from full-time journalism but continues with freelance writing.

1933: Paterson's poetry book for children called *The Animals That Noah Forgot*, illustrated by Norman Lindsay, is published.

1936: *The Shearer's Colt*, Paterson's second novel, is published.

1939: Paterson receives the award of Commander of the British Empire for services to Australian literature.

1941 (5 February): Banjo Paterson dies peacefully, twelve days before his 77th birthday.

1968: A 5c postage stamp with a picture of Banjo Paterson is released by Australia Post. Several other stamps honouring Banjo's poetry and characters are produced in the 1980s and 1990s.

1993: Banjo Paterson is featured on the $10 polymer banknote, with a mob of brumbies being rounded up by a stockman on a horse. The first lines of 'The Man from Snowy River' are printed underneath. The entire poem appears in micro-print as a security feature.

2014: A new set of stamps is released to commemorate the 150th anniversary of Paterson's birth. The poems 'Clancy of the Overflow', 'The Man from Snowy River', 'Waltzing Matilda' and 'Mulga Bill's Bicycle' each feature on a separate stamp.